GLUB!

by Penny Little
illustrated by Sue Mason

ZERO TO TEN

It was Jim's turn to clean out the goldfish bowl.

'Lucky will be quite safe in the kitchen sink,' said Dad, 'just don't forget to put in the plug!'

Lucky didn't much like being
in the sink.
   He looked at Jim fishily.
   'Don't worry,' said Jim,
'your bowl will be sparkling
clean soon.'
   'Glub,' glubbed Lucky.

Jim was drying the clean bowl
when Dad went to get a drink
of water.

He gulped it down, rinsed his
mug, and pulled out the plug.

The water swirled and gurgled
and disappeared ...

'AAAGH!'
Jim stared into the empty sink.
'Where's Lucky?'

Dad skidded into the kitchen.
'OH NO,' he groaned.
'That was my fault ...
he's gone down the plug hole!'

Two big tears plopped onto
Jim's t shirt.

'*Don't worry,*' announced Dad in his
best superhero voice, '*we'll find him!*'

Trapped in the slippery pipe,
Lucky flipped and flapped
and fluttered but he couldn't
get out …

Dad went to the garage to get his tools and Jim peered down the plug hole, but it was too dark to see anything.

'Whatever you do, don't turn on the tap,' called Dad from the garage, 'he'll disappear in the plumbing and ...'

OOOPS! TOO LATE!

Jim had already done it.
A swoosh of water scooped Lucky up
and catapulted him down the pipe ...
Whoooooooosh!

Dad scrambled under the sink with his torch. 'Let's hope that little fish is still in here,' he said to himself as he unscrewed the pipe.

Out flew an old earring, a baby tooth Jim thought he'd swallowed, a clumpy lump of disgusting hairy stuff, and an awful lot of water

...but no fish.

Meanwhile, Lucky was on an underwater roller coaster ride, spinning and twisting ... twirling and swirling. He crossed his fins, closed his eyes and held his breath.

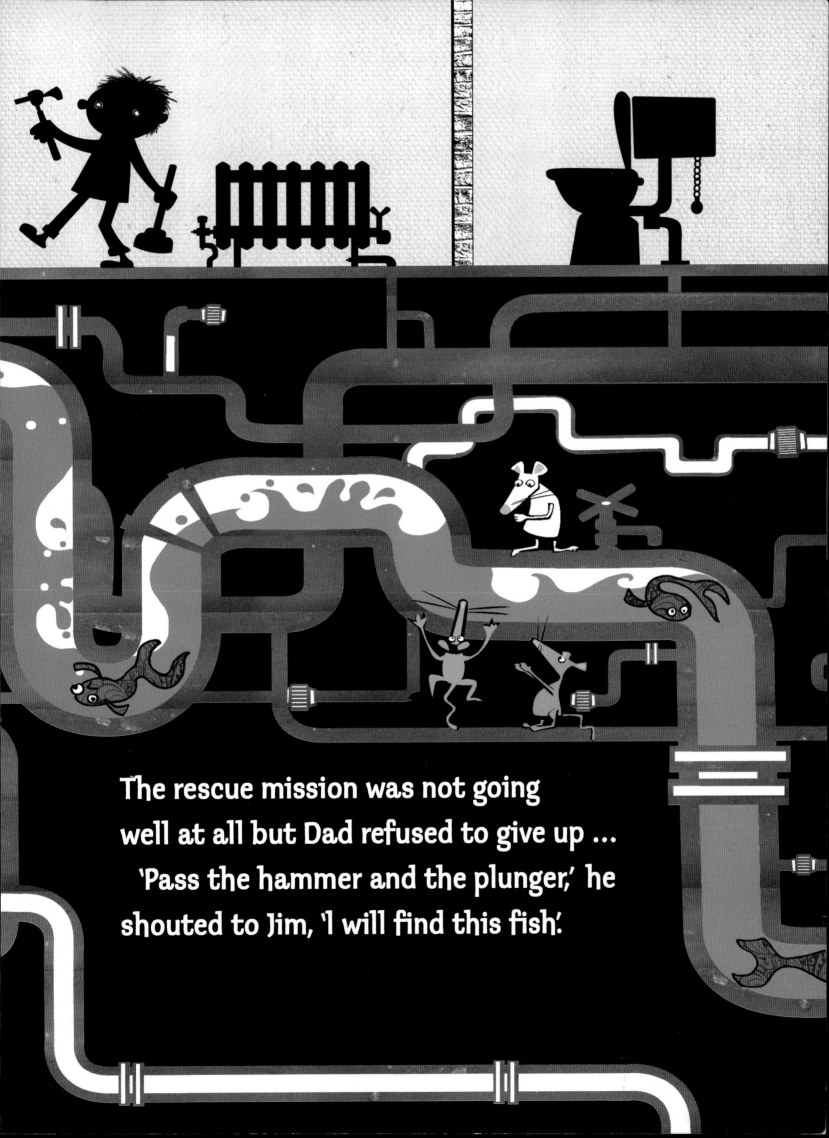

The rescue mission was not going
well at all but Dad refused to give up ...
'Pass the hammer and the plunger,' he
shouted to Jim, 'I will find this fish'.

It was dark and creepy deep in the pipes as the water swooshed him along.

Lucky brushed past something and a shiver of fear prickled down his fish-bone.

He swam away, his heart thumping in his gills.

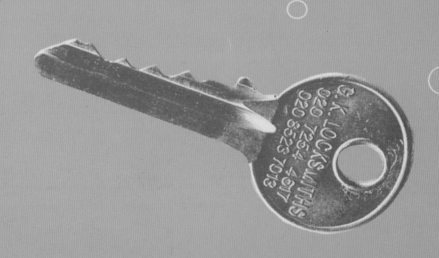

By tea-time Dad had almost put the kitchen sink back together, but there was still no sign of Lucky.

Jim sat on the back doorstep feeling very sad.

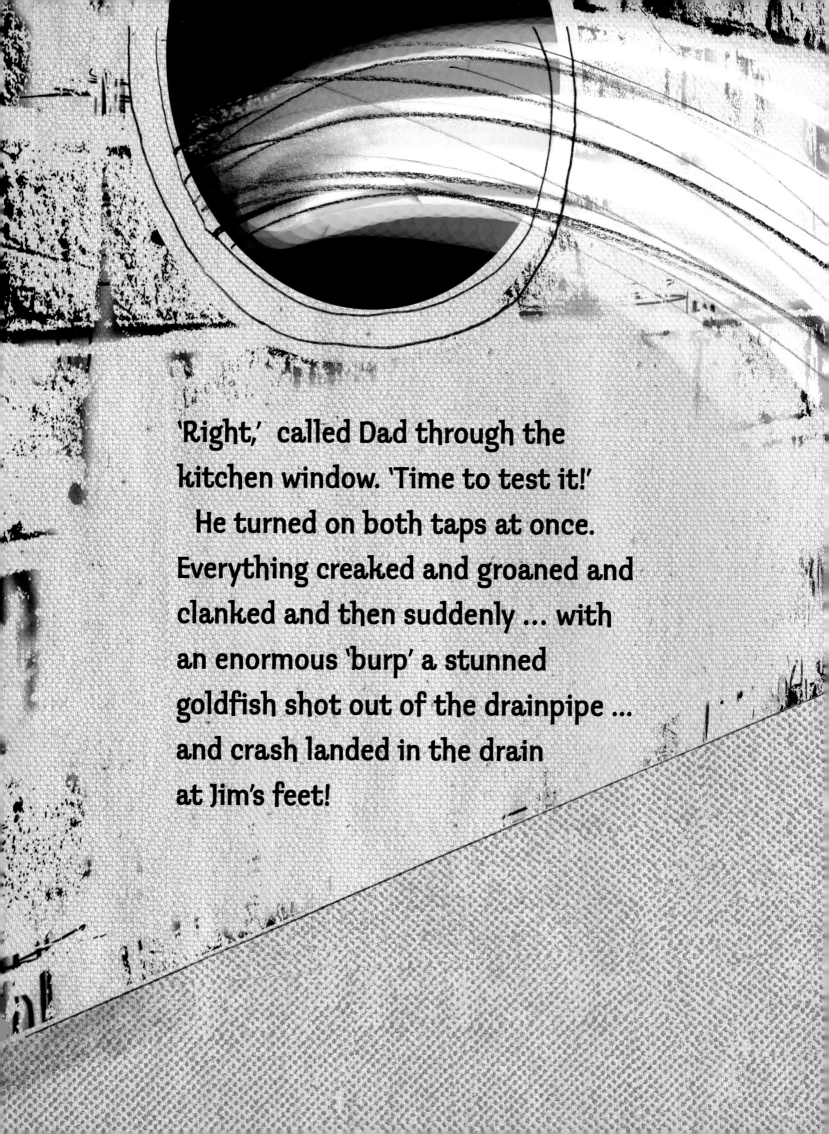

'Right,' called Dad through the
kitchen window. 'Time to test it!'
  He turned on both taps at once.
Everything creaked and groaned and
clanked and then suddenly ... with
an enormous 'burp' a stunned
goldfish shot out of the drainpipe ...
and crash landed in the drain
at Jim's feet!

'LUCKY!' yelled Jim, scooping him
up and popping him in his glass.
'You're alive!'

Lucky goggled Jim in amazement.
'Glub!!!' he glubbed.

'Phew!' said Dad, 'that's a
lucky Lucky!'
  And Jim, too thrilled to speak,
held the glass up to his face and
gave Lucky a gigantic glubby kiss!